My Baby Brother Needs Me

by Jane Belk Moncure
illustrated by Frances Hook

THE
CHILD'S
WORLD

ELGIN, ILLINOIS 60120

Library of Congress Cataloging in Publication Data

Moncure, Jane Belk.
  My baby brother needs me.

  SUMMARY: A young girl describes her baby
brother and how she befriends him.
  [1. Brothers and sisters—Fiction.   2. Babies.
3. Christian life—Fiction]   I. Hook, Frances.
II. Title.
PZ7.M739Mybc 1979b   [E]   79-1074
ISBN 0-89565-070-3

Distributed by Standard Publishing, 8121 Hamilton Avenue,
Cincinnati, Ohio 45231.

My Baby Brother Needs Me

"Let us love one another."

I John 4:7

My baby brother is still so small,
he sleeps a lot,
and hardly cries at all.
I love him.
And I know God loves him too.
I watch him stretch
and kick and crawl.
He is still so small
he needs someone to care for him.

That's what I do.
And I know God cares for him too.

I sing him a song.
Sometimes I sing
about the baby Jesus.
Soon my baby brother
is fast asleep.

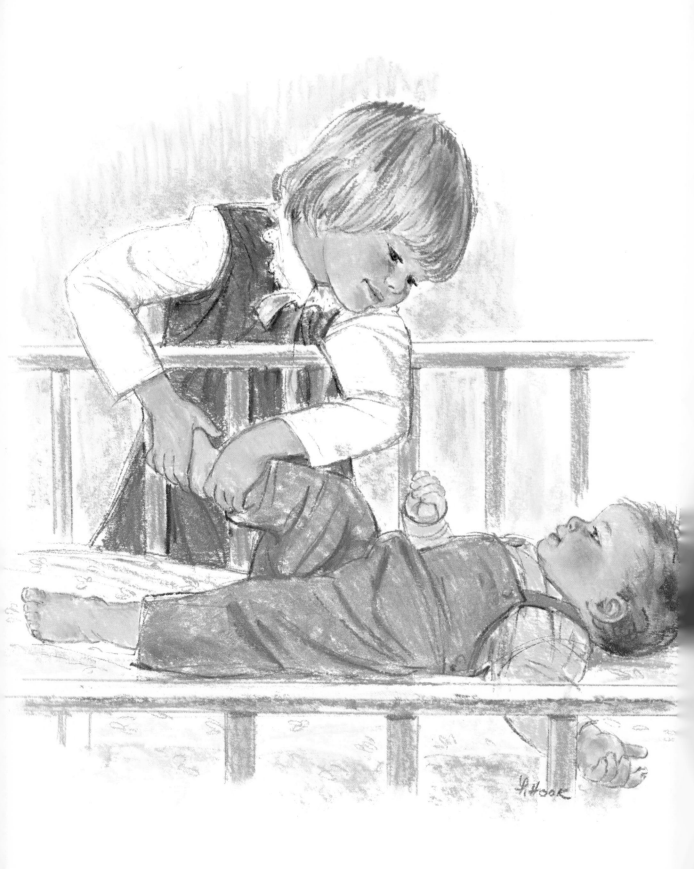

I tickle his toes.
He knows I love him.
And I know God loves him too.

Sometimes I help him take a bath.
He splashes me—
but I just laugh.

Sometimes I take him for a ride.
I tell him about all the things
I see,
because he is still too little
to talk to me.
But he can smile
and say some sounds
and wave.

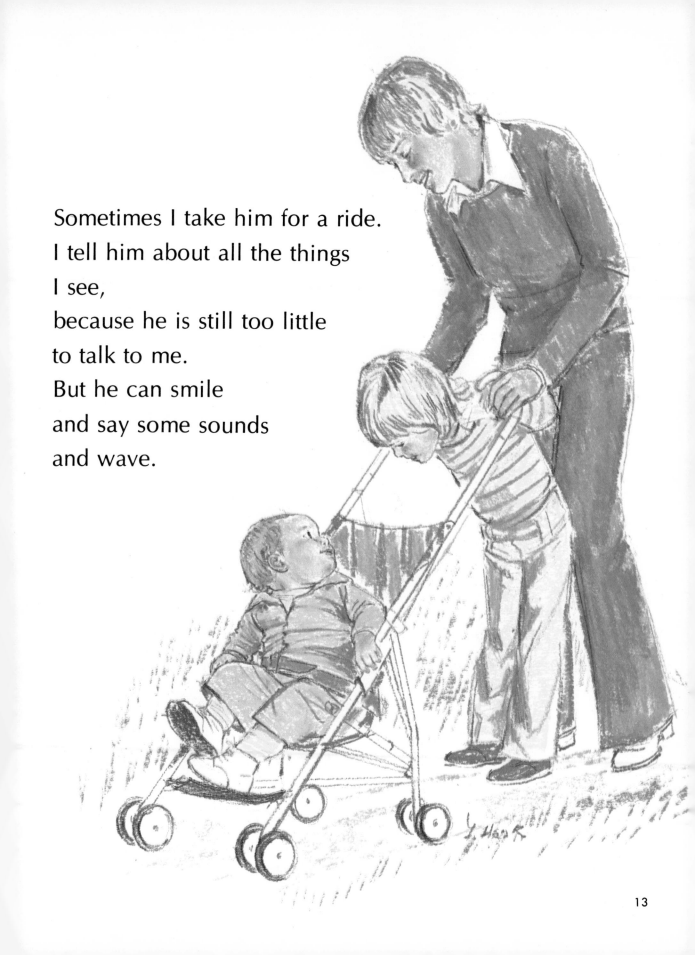

He can fuss and cry.
But when I hold him close,
he smiles again.
He knows I care for him.

Someday he will be big enough
to walk beside me to Sunday school.
But for now,
I will hold him up
and help him stand.

17

When it rains,
he and I will play together
in my room.

19

When it snows,
I will catch snowflakes
for him to hold.

When we go to the zoo,
I will lift him up,
so he can see the animals too.

When we go to the park,
he can ride with me
on the merry-go-round.

He can sit in my lap
and swing.

In spring,
when my birthday comes,
guess what I will do.
I will let him come to my party
and help blow out the candles!

I will give him a piece
of my birthday cake.
You see,
he has never had a birthday
of his own—not yet.
He has never made a wish,
or blown one candle out
or opened a big surprise
from a friend.

He is still so small
he doesn't have many friends.
That's why he needs a friend like me.
I am so thankful for my baby brother.
I love him.
And I know God loves him too.

For David,
who had the chicken pox,
and for Susan,
who told me about it.

I had the chicken pox.

My sister Laura had
the chicken pox.

My brother Paul had
the chicken pox.

Then Daddy got the chicken pox.

Daddy felt sicker than any of us.
He had a fever.
He had a headache.
He had a rash.
He felt sick.
Very sick.

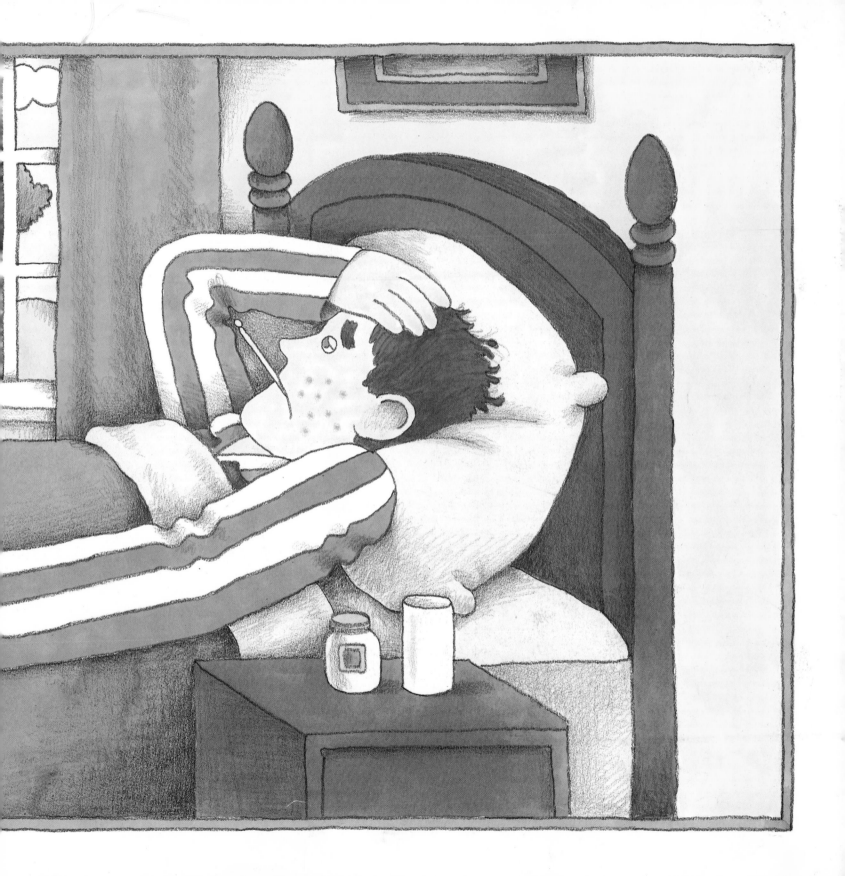

Daddy was too sick to watch TV.
Or read the newspaper.
Or talk on the telephone.

When Mommy brought him lunch, he didn't want it.
Mommy told him he didn't have to eat.
But he had to drink so he wouldn't get dehydrated.

Daddy was supposed to come to my ballet recital.
But he was too sick.
So Mommy came by herself.

I was sad because Daddy couldn't come.
I wished Mommy and Daddy together were
watching me dance.

"When will Daddy get better?" I asked.
"Soon," said Mommy.
"How soon?" I asked.

"Daddy is still getting blisters," Mommy said.
"When he stops getting new ones,
    that's when he'll feel better."

We all wanted to see Daddy's pox.
Mommy said we could—if we didn't make
too much noise, or jump on the bed.
Laura, Paul, and me—we all went into
the bedroom together.

Daddy looked terrible—all covered with pox!
I was scared. I didn't know what to say.
So I held Daddy's hand.
Paul told Daddy he looked funny.
And Laura said, "Yikes!"

Daddy scratched. "I'm itchy!"
I remembered what the doctor told me.
"Don't scratch!" I said. "Or you'll get scars."

Paul said, "Maybe Daddy should have a special bath—just like I did."
"I'll call the doctor and ask," said Mommy.

The doctor thought a bath with oatmeal
might help the itching.
So Mommy filled the tub.
Daddy soaked awhile.
She brought him a towel.
And clean pajamas.

I wanted to help.
But Mommy said no.
I got mad.
So I went to my room and shut the door.

Daddy was sick for four days.
He lay in bed and didn't do anything
except moan and groan.
I was scared Daddy might have to go to the hospital.
I didn't tell anybody how scared I was.
But every night before I went to sleep I
begged for him to get better.
"Let everything be good again," I wished.
"And please don't let Daddy die."

"Would someone find the Sunday paper and bring
it to me?" yelled Daddy from the bedroom.
That's when I knew Daddy must be getting better.

Daddy wanted the newspaper. Then he wanted to watch TV. "Who took the remote control box?" he asked.

Then he wanted his briefcase. And he also wanted a grilled cheese sandwich with bacon and tomato.

I was sure Daddy was better.
So I brought my box of Lego to him.
"Would you help me build?" I asked.
"Sure," said Daddy.
Daddy put away his papers.
"We can build here," he said. "On top of my briefcase."
"Let's make a hospital," I said.
And that's what we did.

The next morning Daddy came to the kitchen for breakfast.
There he was at the table, telling Paul to wipe his mouth
and Laura to finish her cocoa.
"Sit up straight, Ellen," he said to me.
I didn't mind because Daddy was eating with us again.
He wasn't sick!

Then Daddy said, "Ellen, after breakfast,
can we have a ballet recital in the living room?"
"Okay," I said. "I'll get my leotard and tights.

Mommy and Daddy sat together on the sofa.
Paul was the announcer.
Laura turned on the record player.
And I danced.

Everything was good again.